Wont

For C and M

First published in Great Britain by HarperCollins Publishers Ltd in 1996
10 9 8 7 6 5 4 3 2 1
First published in Picture Lions in 1996
10 9
Picture Lions is an imprint of the Children's Division,
part of HarperCollins Publishers Limited
Copyright © Clare Jarrett 1996
The author/illustrator asserts the moral right to be identified as the author/illustrator of the work.
A CIP catalogue record for this book is available from the British Library.
ISBN 0 00 198191-9 (HB)
ISBN 0 00 664595-X (PB)
Printed in Singapore

CATHERINE
AND THE LION

Clare Jarrett

PictureLions
An Imprint of HarperCollins*Publishers*

Catherine woke up and saw the lion.
He was smiling.

"Hello, Lion," she said.

Lion walked over
and sat next to her.

Catherine told him
about her climbing
frame and her new
sister.

"Let's have breakfast," said Catherine.
They went downstairs. Catherine found
an extra large bowl for Lion.

After breakfast she went to get
dressed. She decided to wear her
pink dress with yellow buttons.

She put it on as quickly as she
could. Then she put on her coat.
"Will you come to school
with me?" Catherine asked.

"Yes," said Lion.

She remembered to take
her library book.

At school, she took off her coat and hung it on her peg.

"This way," she whispered and went into the classroom.

"Hello, Catherine," said Mrs Tickle. The children were pleased to see Lion. Catherine sat between Jason and Lauren, and Lion sat behind her.

"Good morning, everyone," said Mrs Tickle.

"Good morning, Mrs Tickle," said the children.

In the big hall Catherine did
cutting and sticking, then painting.
She did a picture of Lion.

At breaktime they skipped and played,
running round and round on the grass.

Lion gave rides.

"I'm thirsty," said Lion.

Catherine found a bowl and
filled it with water for him.

After lunch everybody had a rest.
They all lay on mats while Mrs Tickle
read to them. The afternoon was spent
making things.

Catherine made a golden crown
and gave it to Lion.

"Thank you, Catherine," said Lion.

When it was time to go home,
Catherine gave Lion a big hug.

"I like school," she said.
"So do I," said Lion.

On the way home they did some shopping.
Catherine chose jewels, two silver bracelets
and a diamond ring.

Catherine felt tired. Lion gave her a ride
some of the way.

They played in the garden. Lion rocked
Catherine in the hammock and began to
teach her how to roar.

Soon tea was ready.
It was fish fingers.

"My lion is under the
table," said Catherine.

After tea they watched *ZapCat*,
then it was bathtime.

Lion sat next to the bath
and sniffed the steam.

Catherine wrote LION
on the window.

Lion watched Catherine
put on her pyjamas and
brush her teeth.

"Lions don't have to brush
their teeth," he said.

"Of course they do," said
Catherine. "Everyone does."

"Say goodnight to little sister," said Catherine.

Mum read Catherine a
story, tucked her up and
gave her a big hug and kiss.

"Night, night darling,"
she said. "Sleep tight."
Catherine snuggled down.

"Goodnight Lion. Will
you always be here?"

"Yes I will," said Lion.